W9-CBL-537

DISCARD

TIGHT TIMES

Barbara Shook Hazen

pictures by **Trina Schart Hyman**

The Viking Press   *New York*

JAMES~~~~~~ LIBRARY
OLD OR~~~~~~ BEACH, ME.

VIKING
A Division of Penguin Books USA Inc.
375 Hudson Street, New York, New York 10014
Penguin Books Ltd, 27 Wrights Lane, London W8 5TZ (Publishing & Editorial) and
Harmondsworth, Middlesex, England (Distribution & Warehouse)
Penguin Books Australia Ltd, Ringwood, Victoria, Australia
Penguin Books Canada Limited, 10 Alcorn Avenue, Toronto, Ontario, Canada M4V 3B2
Penguin Books (N.Z.) Ltd, 182-190 Wairau Road, Auckland 10, New Zealand

Text copyright © Barbara Shook Hazen, 1979
Illustrations copyright © Trina Schart Hyman, 1979
All rights reserved
First published in 1979 by The Viking Press
Published simultaneously in Canada
Printed in the United States of America
Set in Plantin
9   10

Library of Congress Cataloging in Publication Data
Hazen, Barbara Shook. Tight times.
Summary: A youngster isn't sure why a thing
called "tight times" means not getting a dog.
[1. Family problems—Fiction] I. Hyman, Trina Schart. II. Title.
PZ7.H314975Ti [E]   78-31867   ISBN 0-670-71287-6

Without limiting the rights under copyright reserved above, no part of this
publication may be reproduced, stored in or introduced into a retrieval
system, or transmitted, in any form or by any means (electronic, mechanical,
photocopying, recording or otherwise), without the prior written permission
of both the copyright owner and the above publisher of this book.

FOR BRACK—
after the tight, the best of times

This morning I asked Mom, Why can't I have a dog?
Not now, she said. Not again.
And not to bother her when she's busy.

So I asked Daddy, Why can't I have a dog? Last year you said I could
have one when I was bigger. And I'm a lot bigger, see? So why not now?

Because of tight times, said Daddy.
He said I was too little to understand.

I'm not too little, I said.

Daddy said he'd give me a shoulder ride
and tell me all about it at breakfast.

He said tight times are when everything keeps going up.

I had a balloon that did that once.

Daddy said tight times are why we all eat Mr. Bulk instead of cereals in little boxes.

I like little boxes better.

Daddy said tight times are why we went to the sprinkler last summer instead of the lake.

I like the lake better.

Daddy said tight times are why we don't have a roast beef on Sunday.
Instead we have soupy things with lima beans. I hate lima beans.
If I had a dog, I'd make him eat mine.

Daddy said tight times are why Mrs. McIntosh picks me up after school instead of Mommy, because of Mommy's job.

Mommy was more fun.

Mrs. McIntosh isn't good at games and she never wants to watch what I want on TV. I'd trade her for a dog any day.

JAMESON SCHOOL LIBRARY
OLD ___ ___ BEACH, ME.

This afternoon something funny happened. Daddy came home in the middle of the day. I was making up a new game and Mrs. McIntosh was watching her program.

Daddy looked mad. He said something to Mrs. McIntosh and she left.

Then Daddy fixed us both special drinks. He said he wasn't mad at me. He said he was mad because he'd lost something.

I said look behind the radiator because that's where I found my lost puzzle piece.

Daddy said it wasn't that simple. What he'd lost was his job.

Then Mommy came home. She gave me a candy bar and said she wanted to talk to Daddy.

She said I could go outside and sit on the front steps. But not to go near the street, no matter what.

Mrs. McIntosh never let me do that!

I was just sitting on the steps when I heard something.
It sounded like it was coming from the trash can. It sounded like someone crying.
It kept on crying. So I walked over and looked under the lid.

There was something in there. It was a cat. I don't know how it got in but a nice lady helped me get it out. I never saw such a skinny little cat!

I gave it some of my candy bar, but it wouldn't eat. The nice lady said to give it a saucer of milk.

I asked the lady if it was her cat. She said no. She said I could keep it if I wanted.

Wow, what a nice lady!

I ran all the way up the stairs.

I tiptoed into the kitchen. I tried to be quiet. But the milk
was up too high. It tipped and made a terrible mess.

Mommy and Daddy ran out of their room. Daddy looked funny.
He looked at the cat. Then he looked at me.

What's that! he asked.

It's a cat, I told him. A nice lady said I could keep it.
And I didn't go near the street.

Then something sort of scary happened. Daddy started to cry. So did Mommy.

I didn't know daddies cried. I didn't know what to do.

Then they both made a sandwich hug with me in the middle. So I started to cry.

Then Daddy said, Okay, okay, you can keep it. Only one thing—
I never want to hear another word about your wanting a dog, ever!
Okay, I said.

After dinner Daddy asked me what I was going to call my cat.
Dog, I said, because I always wanted one, even if I don't any more.

Dog's a great cat. She's good at games and she likes to tickle me with her chin whiskers.

I sure hope Dog likes lima beans.

E
HAZ

Hazen, Barbara Shook

Tight times

C·2

$14.99

DATE			
6/9/94			
8/24 Sh			

JAMESON SCHOOL LIBRARY

OLD ORCHARD BEACH, ME.

BAKER & TAYLOR BOOKS